NOVELS BY D.M. DE ALWIS

PAWN OF SAMSARA DUOLOGY
A Lion's Head
A Lion's Pride

SHORT STORIES
A Water Horse

A Monkey's Mask (forthcoming)

A Water Horse

The Lament of Saoirse

By D.M. De Alwis

Copyright @ 2026 by D.M. De Alwis

The Lament of Saoirse

For more information, visit **www.dmdealwis.com**

ISBN 978-1-0696660-3-1 (Paperback)
First Edition: 2026

Editing by EMSA Publishing, Elise Abram
Cover design by D. Corlosquet
Illustration by Luke McAnuff

Published by Ahasae Tharu Publishing, Toronto, Canada

For mothers.

A Haon

Saoirse refused to bear witness to her sister, Eimear's, marriage to the old, withered chieftain of *Cuan.* He had married six times prior without an heir. Little did the chieftain know that Eimear had already enjoyed the company of a lad from her father's garrison. Saoirse had no doubt Eimear would deliver a child to the chieftain.

"Your turn will be next. You cannot mistake the way Fintan looks at you." Eimear squeezed Saoirse's cheek until it hurt. In return, Saoirse looked into Eimear's sharp hazel eyes—said to be identical to her own—with what she hoped was burning defiance. She wove a green ribbon into her sister's fair hair. Eimear wore a long, thick, felted wool gown of dark grey—more of the green ribbon served as both a belt and adornment. As was custom, the loosely tied knots were elaborate, requiring the bridegroom to work for his reward of bedding the bride.

"I will find a way to escape my fate," Saoirse said. She fought off the despair of a sinking heart. Why couldn't she be more like Eimear, accepting her privilege and fate? She would find no sympathy from her family.

Saoirse broke away from her sister. She blinked away the tears welling up in her eyes. In her mind, she replayed the scenes from their childhood together: playing in the tall grasses, hunting deer by moonlight, and retelling spooky stories of the fae during heavy rains. She feared that, just as her other sisters and mother before them, she would never see her sister again. Eimear walked a different path while she was left behind.

Saoirse kissed her sister goodbye. "I wish you good health and a long life, my sister." She watched from the back of her dappled mare as the bride train left for the marches in the West. She watched as they moved at a snail's pace between the stone walls that lined their route—enough men to protect her from any danger. Eimear was still a free woman, but for the yoke of responsibility as a Chieftain's wife. She would have one child while young and live the remainder of her life as a privileged chieftain's wife. Eimear would do well by her husband.

Saoirse had a high degree of freedom as the High Lord Tyrone's youngest daughter. She exercised her right to hunt and ride. She was rewarded with nods of approval from the elders who whispered, "Strong women birth strong sons." For Saoirse, weakness was not an option. She believed the act of childbirth was more apt to end the lives of women. After years of blessing Lord Tyrone with children, her mother had been granted her request to live in a small stone cottage with her younger children. Her mother had lived until both she and her youngest son died of childbirth sickness. Saoirse had seen her ninth summer solstice when Eimear had come at a run to tell her the news. With their younger brothers sent for fosterage, the two remaining sisters were brought to live in the cold stone fort, the main residence of their father's estates.

Saoirse pined for a return to her simpler life. She could no longer bear the thought of living in a dank, dark, stone fort with the stench of the garrison holding guard. Her freedom to ride and hunt was bound to be replaced by crying infants and a never-ending list of household duties.

Her brothers had been free to roam or settle down as they liked. Their father, the High Lord Tyrone, was well into his prime, holding good relations with the druids and the High Kings of Eriu, Banba, and Fodla. He had convinced his six older daughters to marry and forge political ties. Saoirse's brothers had been raised well, adhering to a higher order of reasoning. They were well-tempered, well-bred, and kept to a high moral standard. As such, Tyrone's clan would grow stronger. Seeing her sisters wed one by one to brutish but powerful men, Saoirse could only assume her fate would be the same.

She was not married yet.

Desiring an escape, Saoirse rode her dappled mare through dense forest to the long-abandoned emerald green fields of Ceide. Her mare was content to feast on the lush clover and fresh rye grass. She tethered the mare to a tree and found a hidden space under the boughs of another great tree. Then, she gathered firewood while she waited until dark to confirm local suspicions.

Here she allowed herself to weep. Had Eimear been here, she would say, "No one would be daft enough to stalk a fairy ring at night." Nevertheless, her sister had accompanied Saoirse on wild rides—though never after dark. Her sister was not here to call her foolish, nor to remind her that to receive the attention of the Aes Sídhe was dangerous. In all her time searching, they had never found anything to prove the druid's stories true. "A bit of harmless fun," Saoirse would say.

Through tears, Saoirse sensed a shift in the shadows and moonlight. Looking up, she saw green-blue lights hovering and dancing in a circle around the massive faerie ring. She hesitated a moment before standing up to circle it. What were they? Would she be transported to another realm only to return in a hundred years? Was that what she wanted? She edged closer. She entered the field. Should she have come during the full moon?

Rain began to fall. Saoirse felt her courage build. She took a deep breath and leaped into the circle. Nothing happened.

The lights continued to swirl around her. They moved away from her palm when she sought to touch them.

Will-o'-the-wisps.

She closed her eyes and let herself sway and dance in the rain. She imagined herself dancing with the fairies. She was exhausted, cold, wet, and breathing hard when she finished.

Having gathered wood before her foray, she lit a bonfire as the sun set behind the ancient forest. The light banished the dark, leaving the pitch-black halo that was the forest around her. She was blind to the night in her cocoon of light. Her mind went numb as she stared into the dancing orange-gold flames. Her clothing dried as the hot air warmed her bones and buffeted her golden locks.

The fire burned down to embers as dawn touched the sky. In the dark, she rode her mare past sleeping homesteads. She kept an arrow nocked in her bow. Caution was expected, though she did not have to worry about the company she kept. "Saoirse, Tyrone's daughter," was all she needed to say as identification. None in the region would dare lay a finger to harm her head.

All she wanted was a simple life: The freedom to enjoy a sunrise. Time to discover the bogs and hills. In this birth, she was ruled by men seeking power, fame, or wealth, who would use her as a broodmare. Her fate would be to die in childbirth, like her mother. She wished nothing more than to escape. Her children need not be pawns to nobility.

A dutiful daughter, Saoirse returned to the estate for several days and nights of sleep and preparation for her father's annual banquet. High Lord Tyrone had earned his title by forging peace with the druids some twenty years past, when the men of the land began cutting the dense forest. Men and women from the region had brought their wares and given vows of fealty. In exchange, they were gifted an allotment of grain, meat, or provisions—a means of sharing the abundance of the land with everyone, whether they were a farmer, fisherman, or craftsman.

The Southern field had been cleared for the feast. A full moon, twinkling stars, and burning torches provided sufficient light. Bonfires were tended at regular intervals to cook and serve spits of wild boar, venison, and game fowl. A bed of coals had been prepared to roast fish and cockles. Great cauldrons held soup and stews. Plenty of volunteers offered their help in preparation for the feast. Everyone in the region attended. The High Lord's table was the only one that stood under an awning so naught would fall on the heads or in the food of those seated. There sat Tyrone, his second wife, Sorcha, his heirs, and advisers.

Saoirse was grateful for an event held outside—inside, the stench of unwashed bodies and stale ale clung to the air. She sipped her cup of mead and observed several bards taking turns, regaling the crowd with bawdy or scary tales. During one rare silence, she heard the horses and donkeys tethered in the distance for the night. By morning, people would have found a soft patch of grass or a pasture and wrapped themselves in cloaks for rest. Latrines had been dug downhill, but the stench wafted like a ghostly spectre as the winds changed course. Not that most of the guests knew how to use the latrines.

Saoirse pinched her nose, grateful for the rosemary nosegay she had tied to her wrist.

"Greetings." She looked up to find a tall, ginger-haired and beardless fellow standing before her. "Is this seat taken?"

Saoirse shook her head in response and waved down a server.

"I can't pass up a free meal," he said. She noted his strange accent. He hailed a friend from the crowd, dark-haired, with a long face. He brought with him a plate, brimming with venison. "Ooh! Roasted to perfection!"

She ignored her company and continued eating her plate of cockles. A coven of druid lore masters was also in attendance. Saoirse had served them the special bread, soup, and water her father's cooks had prepared to order before taking her seat. She was enthralled by the lore master as he took his turn from the bards and sang a tale accompanied by bodhrán and pipe.

He sang of the shapeshifters, the each-uisge, and the kelpie, both water spirits. The former were the rage-filled destroyers of ships, whereas the latter lured their victims to die in rivers and lochs.

"Beware, beware . . . beware the shapeshifters above the High King's law." He sang a song of how a kelpie maiden had shape-shifted to steal the heart of the High King's son and lured him to his watery grave.

As the song ended, the High King's son, Fintan,

in attendance, bellowed, "It's true. It's all true. That's exactly how it ended. If only my great-great-cousin had burned the bracken he had picked from her hair, she would have lost her ability to change back."

The two gents at her table guffawed. She frowned at them and rose, intending to thank the lore master for his song.

The copper-haired man caught her by the hand. She glared at him, but he only smiled without guile. "I would that we could meet," he said. She looked at him for the first time, noting his chiselled jaw, pointed nose, and soft, sea-green eyes. "I'm Conor."

"Perhaps another time," she replied. She pulled away her hand just as her father, High Lord Tyrone, stood upon the dais and announced he had chosen his daughter's betrothed. Cheering erupted.

"Where are you, my youngest daughter?" he called.

"Here!" she raised her hand. A pathway opened in the crowd, and she walked to the dais. Standing beside her father was Fintan, the High King's seventh son, who clamped his sweaty bear paw over her hand. The room erupted in shouts, cheers, and the thunder of a hundred wooden cups drumming against the wooden tabletop.

They would be wed at the next full moon.

Fintan smelled of the drink. Saoirse wondered when he had last bathed. Revulsed, she tried to free her hand from his grasp, only for him to draw her closer. His lips were fixed with a drunken smile of contentment as he gazed upon her with satisfaction through half-closed lids. He hugged her tightly to his chest, oblivious to her revulsion.

She eyed the coagulated gravy and bits of bread in his ratty beard. He burped loudly. The foul cloud made her feel faint. She put two hands on his chest and pushed while taking one step backward.

At least, he took direction. Though he lost his balance as he let her go and stepped backward into the melee of departing guests. She twirled on her heels, adeptly wove through the crowd of revellers, and out to the stables and her mare.

Saoirse rode her mare to the Drombeg stone circle. She carried with her provisions enough to last a fortnight. Blissfully alone, she created a nest at its centre. There, she slept for three days, spending the daytime praying to the ancients to show her a way out of her predicament. "Please, Tuatha Dé Danann, take pity on me and give me guidance!"

A Dó

In the morning, a continuous breeze blew from the land to the sea, drawing her footsteps to the seashore. She walked from the stones to the sandy beach and removed her shoes before reaching the flat sand left by the waves. Feeling bold, she stripped off her fur-lined mantle, dress, and leine, her knee-length, sleeveless tunic, and walked into the grey sea. The icy cold waters washed away her anxiety. The water was not too deep, the waves lapping. She dove under the waters and listened to the waves on the surface as the water caressed her bare skin. She felt free.

Satisfied, she dressed in her leine, combed her long blonde hair, and allowed it to dry in the sun.

"T'will be a grand thing, indeed, to bed thee." Fintan's voice came from the dunes.

"How are you here?" Saoirse reached for a weapon she did not have.

"I sent a man to follow ye, Saoirse. I only arrived this morning. They say a man should show interest in his wife's affairs." Fintan's heavy footsteps marred the wind-swept sand as he stepped from the dune to the beach. Shedding his mantle and clothes, he ran naked into the cold waters.

"We're not married yet," she said.

"I don't see what ye find desirable in these frigid waters," he said as he returned. His starch-white skin took on a red pallor from the cold. At least he was washed, but she would not hide her disdain for him.

"Ye don't want to marry me."

"I don't," she said.

He frowned.

"Did you come alone?" she asked.

"My men are at the Drombeg. They tell me to beware the woman who dances in faerie rings . . . that she be a sorceress tempting the fae."

"And if I am?"

"A suitable wife, ye shall not make," he said. He dusted the sand off his feet before pulling up his breeches. "Or, perhaps, ye will be very suitable. I am an ambitious man, seventh in line to the throne. Those superstitious fools count me as special . . . t'would give the druids something to sing."

The waves suddenly picked up and crashed hard against the shore, startling her. The unnatural wave crept its way up the sand to lap at Fintan's feet. He cursed and rushed to pick up the rest of his clothes before they were soiled.

"Sorceress!"

"That wasn't me," she said, "but I fear you have

brought something upon us." She could not believe her eyes: a magnificent chestnut stallion had risen from the agitated waters as if by magic. She blinked and rubbed her eyes as it stood its ground, staring back at her.

"Stay back!" Fintan had found his sword in the muddle of his things. Hands shaking, he pointed it at the horse. "An each-uisge! I will not be . . . not be . . . ruled by you."

The stallion boldly stepped forward, rearing up on two legs and took two hops toward him, causing Fintan to drop his sword and back away.

"Come away, Saoirse!"

She would not. Saoirse took two steps toward the fearsome beast. When she reached up her cautious hand, palm out, it snorted sea spray. The stallion was taller than any horse she had ever seen. The sea horse bowed its head and lay down on its quarters, docile. She dared reach up and touch it between its eyes—It felt solid enough.

"Hello, handsome, I'm Saoirse." In a dream-like state, she could hear Fintan screaming at her from the dunes. She had sought magic for so long. An idea sprang into her head. This would be her escape, with Fintan as witness.

With a knowing smile, she glanced over at him before mounting the stallion, bareback.

"*Níl!* Saoirse!" Fintan's words were lost to the wind rushing in her ears. The moment she found her place, the horse leaped up and ran. Saoirse held onto his thick mane in a panic, but as he raced away from Fintan, she realized she would not fall. Her legs were somehow transfixed to the creature's body. The sea horse's mane was littered with bracken and sand as if he had been rolling on the bottom of the sea floor.

The stallion turned a right angle and ran into the surf. They were running over water. Saoirse felt fear as she watched the black water and waves rush past. They were going out to sea. She would die a watery death.

A calm descended over her. So be it, she willed. She would rather die than assume life on land with Fintan. She rode the each-uisge across the waves. By nightfall, she had grown faint, not only from fatigue, but also from hunger. When she finally lost consciousness, she barely registered that they had returned to their starting point.

She woke up on the beach, tucked under her warm mantle. The waves crashed against the shore, but, as if by magic, she had been spared the wet tide. Two men wrestled by the sea. The taller had hair a hue of orange that matched the setting sun, falling in stringy, wet locks. The shorter man was dark, his black hair gathered in an untidy bun. They ran and played in the waves, swimming and coming to the shore, digging their feet in the sand like children. She enjoyed the abandon with which they played. She recognized them then. These shapeshifters were the same two men she had met at her father's gathering. The tall, copper-haired fellow had introduced himself as Conor. An idea began to form in her head as she watched. Quietly, she dressed and, leaving her mantle behind as a sign that she would return, left the beach.

Fintan and his men had left the Drombeg. Her mare was nowhere to be seen, though she thanked the Goddess that the superstitious fools had left her nest untouched. She found her provisions and her bow.

By sunset, she had returned to the empty beach carrying a deer she had shot with a bow and arrow. Leaving the deer on the beach, she made countless trips to gather enough wood for a bonfire and a spit. Then, she sat in the dimming light to clean and spit the venison. Saoirse turned the spit to the sound of the ocean waves. The smell of venison would make for an incredible lure.

"Conor!" She greeted the one she assumed was her rescuer when they rose from the sea. He approached brightly, with delight, while his companion wore a sullen expression.

"This is my brother . . . call him Eric. May we join you?"

"Be welcome each-uisge. I wish to thank you." By the time the venison had been cooked, they had exchanged more than pleasantries. The two each-uisge sat in their human forms, eating comfortably. Saoirse took a seat between them. From this close, she could see the sea bracken woven through Conor's hair. While telling stories and idly chatting, she absently picked the bracken from his hair. When he showed no sign of complaint, she continued.

"I dance in the light, yet hold no form. With the sun, I grow, but in the dark, I'm born, elusive and fleeting in the Eriu morn," said Eric. Waves crashed against the shore as a lone wolf cried out in the distance.

"Are you a shadow?" Saoirse clapped her hands.

Conor looked up at her from where his head was cradled in her lap. "I have one," he said. "A guardian of the night with a silvery glow, over the land my phases show. I wane and wax but never grow."

"That's easy: you're the moon," she replied. She boldly tweaked his nose. She had managed to clear his hair of the bracken, but the sand remained.

"We should go," Eric said, looking wistfully at the sea. "Cailleach Bhéara is waiting."

"You go. I'm going to keep company with Saoirse." Conor held her hands and turned them over as he inspected them in the firelight. Eric shrugged and stalked off into the darkness.

Saoirse continued to run her fingers through Conor's hair. The sand was hard to dislodge, but the fire's heat helped dry it. The tiny grains dried and fell to the beach. By morning, she had worked his head free of any trace of the sea. He lay asleep in her arms.

"Conor," she whispered. "Conor, come inland with me."

"I will." His sea-green eyes studied her face. He rose and took her hand. She led him from the beach and up the sandy dunes into the forest. She whistled. Her mare came at a run.

"Ride with me," she said.

"Sure, I will," he said.

With Conor by her side, Saoirse would have company on the long nights. She rode off with Conor without another thought. Her mind raced to find a remote location where they could live far away from the sea and any body of water.

A Trí

The first year was the hardest. Conor, an able student, followed her like a puppy. He was an amiable man. He let her decide where they lived and the layout of their home. They claimed an abandoned stone cottage surrounded by a partially built stone wall, inland, in a wild, long-abandoned stretch of rolling hills. She had to teach him the ways of living, such as hunting, maintaining a fire, and cooking. Often, she would find him staring vacantly in the direction of the sea. In those worrisome moments, she tried to distract him. Their playful moments gave way to flirtation and relations. She was determined to seduce him into a state of forgetfulness.

Despite her fears, Saoirse gave birth to a child. They named him Nolan. Conor's attention to his offspring was the final, vital ingredient to the spell she had cast: he doted on their fair, blue-eyed son.

As the years passed, Saoirse worried less that Conor would stray. In the early years, she would leave Conor behind to mind the homestead while their infant was in tow. Skirting the small towns and villages, she would ride to the larger cities where anonymity would allow her to trade for necessary provisions. Saoirse continued to ride her mare and to hunt. They watched their Nolan grow from infant to toddler. A child with a fondness for water, he would dance when it rained. He learned to shoot a bow. She taught him to sing.

She was grateful for the hand Conor played in raising their son, as she could range further from their home in search of game for days at a time.

On these occasions, Nolan and Conor would intuit her return and be waiting for her. One day, when Nolan had seen nine summer solstices, she arrived to find them absent from the gates. Seeing smoke billowing from the chimney, she tended to her mare and donkey while worries formed in her mind. Perhaps Nolan was ill or had come to harm. Neither of them came out to meet her in the shed. Alone, she unloaded the deer and carried it to the smokehouse.

The front door opened to the warmth of a roaring fire. There was Nolan, well and whole, seated on the braided rug and playing with some small thing. The room was dark. As her eyes adjusted to the dim, smoky room, she found Conor seated on her short stool in conversation with a man, his back revealing only his woollen shift.

His black hair was tied in a messy knot.

"Saoirse, this is my brother, Eric," Conor said by way of introduction.

"Eric," Saoirse touched the man's arm as he stood and turned around. She had brought enough game for the incoming winter. The name seemed familiar to her. Recognition and unease set in. "Good that I have brought venison."

"That is most kind, it has been awhile," Eric said. "I spent years searching for ye, Conor."

"Did we not leave on friendly terms?"

"We did not." Eric smiled, but not with his eyes.

"Ma! He brought me this!" Nolan pushed a large, empty conch shell into his mother's face.

Saoirse was finally met with bear hugs and kisses from Conor and Nolan.

"Ma, I was setting snares for rabbits when he appeared," said Nolan.

A short time later, Conor accompanied Nolan to see to the outside chores, leaving Saoirse with Eric, who sat on their only bench with a mug of nettle tea. "Do *you* remember me? For it appears my brother does not," he said.

She felt the hair on the back of her neck rise. "I'm sorry. I'm so sorry." Saoirse fell to her knees and clasped her hands. "Please forgive me. I wanted to live my life."

Eric rose and stood, looking down at her. "And you don't think he wanted to live his life? What kind of life is this?" he asked.

"He is happy!" she said.

"Aye. You gave him a son. Anyone would be happy to have a child. What did you do to him that he has forgotten his brother and the sea?"

"Naught," she stood up and backed away.

Nolan burst in through the door, followed closely by Conor. She composed herself and felt grateful when Eric seemed happy to feign they had no animosity between them.

Conor looked between his wife and his brother. "One big happy family," he said. He served them a dinner of roasted potatoes and stewed rabbit.

"But you live dreadfully far from the sea," Eric said.

"We do. I would very much like to take Nolan to the sea," Conor said. His words caused Saoirse to grip her trencher, her mind racing for an argument to dissuade him.

"Does Nolan even know how to swim?"

"I can teach him!"

"Níl! I mean, what if he were to drown?" Saoirse asked, fear rising in her throat.

"I can assure you, Nolan will never drown while I am alive," Eric replied.

"That sorts it," Conor continued, "we go to the sea tomorrow."

"Can I, Ma?" Nolan said.

Saoirse did not have the heart to refuse Nolan. She loved her son as much as she had grown to love Conor. They were her family.

She looked at Eric with pleading eyes, only to be met with cold disregard.

The tasteless meal stuck in her throat. "As is your uncle's will, Nolan." She swallowed hard.

That night, Saoirse clung tightly to Conor. She worried it would be their last night together. Would he see the sea and leave her? Would he kill her as revenge for taking him away from his first love?

She awoke, gasping after having drowned in her dreams. She could see Eric's cold smile and hear Fintan's obnoxious laughter.

"I've missed you," Conor whispered as he held her close. She wished she could believe it.

After preparing provisions, they left the house shuttered. Conor and Saoirse rode her mare. Eric and Nolan rode the donkey. With every step toward the sea, Saoirse became more anxious.

"Perhaps we should turn around?" Conor offered. She shook her head. A hundred ancient tales of water spirits committing murder haunted her thoughts.

When they stopped for lunch, she hugged Nolan close for comfort.

Rounding a bend in the forest, they heard the sea. Conor's steps picked up, and he ran the mare the last of the steps. Gazing at the immense blue waters, Nolan shouted victoriously and ran for the beach. He stopped short of the waves. Saoirse felt her knees go weak. She couldn't bear to lose her family. She couldn't go back. She feared the cold look behind Eric's eyes.

"Saoirse, wife, up you go!" Conor lifted her and threw her over his shoulder, running with her into the waves. She was crying.

"Hey, hey, what is going on here?"

"You're going to leave me. You're going to go back to the sea."

"We're *in* the sea, Saoirse," he said. His hands forced her face to look up into his sea-green eyes. "I chose you, Saoirse. I followed you. I permitted you to take the bracken from my hair. I went inland with you." He kissed her silent lips with passion.

"Woman, don't you know I fell in love with you long before I saw you bathing at the seashore?" He lifted her above the waves and held her. "I love you, Saoirse! I want to be with no one but you."

For the first time, it dawned on her that she might not be the only one in control of their relationship. She struggled to breathe as relief washed over her.

"Conor, you think you'd have said something." Her words were faint. "I thought I was going to lose you."

"I didn't want to give you any cause for worry, Saoirse," he said. "Don't you know it was hard enough for me to convince you to take me with you, love me, and start a family?"

She shivered suddenly, aware that they stood knee-deep in the cold water.

"Ma! Da! Look here!" Nolan shouted. His parents looked to see him standing in the waves with sand and seaweed in his hair. He dove into the waves.

"Boy is a natural—what did I tell you?" Eric smiled.

"Will Eric ever forgive me for taking you away from the sea?" Saoirse asked Conor.

"He might. You are under my protection from the sea. Perhaps, if we move our home closer to the sea, he may, in time, forgive you."

They could not move house right away. Ten years was a long time to have set down roots. Saoirse and Conor lived a simple, independent life, growing, hunting, or making all they needed.

They did not share their valley with anyone. Saoirse had kept one more secret from Conor over the years: she worried about being found out by her father, High Lord Tyrone. She worried they would encounter more of her people closer to the shore, where the fish and food were abundant. She did not know how to tell Conor this when he walked with a skip in his step.

He, Eric, and Nolan searched for a new place to call home. At least, they were mindful of keeping their anonymity. This was a country where everyone knew everyone else's business. That Saoirse and Conor had managed to vanish into the countryside was pure luck.

"How did you find us?" Saoirse asked Eric one evening after he had begun to warm to her. "I never asked—what gave us away?" She sat near the hearth with Nolan asleep, his head in her lap, a sheepskin keeping him warm against the cool evening air. She hummed a lullaby as she gently detangled his long hair.

"The midwife who attended you ten years ago. I had the luck to shelter with her after rescuing her fisherman husband from a tempest. She told me of a man with a keen resemblance to me and his wife and child." Eric sat further back from the fire and shucked oysters. The door was open, allowing a cool evening breeze to flow through the small, round house and draw the wood smoke out through the hole in the roof.

"I trust she has told no one else of us?"

"Why are you so concerned? No one would suspect my brother of being fae," he replied.

"My people may be looking for me." Saoirse did not expect the look of sympathy he gave her.

"We have more in common than I thought." Conor carried an armload of firewood in through the open door. Conscious of the sleeping Nolan, he stacked the wood quietly by the fire to dry. "I owe a debt to Cailleach Bhéara, the sea hag. There's more than one reason I was content to live here for so long. That day on the beach when we met would have been my last day of freedom."

"You two were long gone when she found out. She wrought a terrible tempest that lasted for months," Eric said. "I told her you were seduced by a *cailín álainn,* a human."

"Would that be enough?" Conor sat down next to Saoirse and pulled her close. Saoirse felt her heart might burst with contentment.

"There is a new harbour, out near Cuan. Sea-going vessels rest there. Perhaps we move there?" Eric asked. "I am sure we would go unhindered. Would any of your father's people recognize you today, Saoirse?"

"They would, indeed. I'd rather not risk it."

"What if we were to take a ship and sail away?" Conor asked.

"Away from Eriu? I don't know if I could survive such a voyage," she said.

"With an each-uisge, your husband, and your son for company, why not, my Saoirse?"

Saoirse could not shake the feeling of dread, but she could find no argument either. She had bound Conor to the land for ten wonderful years.

With a heavy heart, she gave her assent.

Their departure from Cuan had been unremarkable. Eric had drawn gold bars from the sea floor and, with Conor, brokered a ship and the men to man it. Conor's second mate would be a strapping, experienced seaman named Kieran. Saoirse suspected there were more each-uisge hidden among the crew. She could not discern, as many tied their hair back in linen kerchiefs.

The seas were calm as they set out. The land of the Britons to the south and the east was days away. The ship hugged the shore for safety.

The weight of knowing sat on Saoirse's shoulders. The dread of knowing all could end at a moment's notice. She spent her days doting on her son and her husband. Eric was hiding a dark secret, she was sure of it. She did not trust that he had her best interest at heart. He, in turn, was an able and willing uncle to her son.

The night of the full moon, the seas went still. Naught a breeze blew to push sail. Conor joked that the men would need to whittle oars from the mast. Kieran, the rattled first mate, stared out at the horizon. "Has anyone angered the Cailleach Bhéara?" he asked. "The sea stills for no one but she."

Eric and Conor shifted uneasily.

"Nolan, my son, go below decks and strap yourself in," Saoirse said. "Eric, you know what is going on. You know more than you have let on—is this a trap for Conor?"

"I'm sorry, brother," Eric said. "It is a trap for the cailín álainn."

"What have you done?" Conor rushed to Saoirse's side and held her tight. "My love, I will make this right."

"It's okay, Conor," she said, though fear had seized her heart. "Eric, what did you promise her?"

"I did not know you then"—Eric bowed his head—"Saoirse."

"That is no excuse!" Conor, a dangerous look in his eye, rounded on his brother. "Make it right. What can we do to make it right?"

"She wants blood," he replied. "She wants you banished from these lands and seas. I have a plan. We can go to the far south." He looked at Saoirse before continuing. "Nolan will be safe."

"How do we move without wind or waves, man?" Kieran shouted. The crew was tying themselves down securely as the leaders talked. A squall had appeared in the East.

"Conor, protect Nolan. Please, go to him. I love you. I have always loved you. Just go. She wants me." Tears streamed from Saoirse's eyes. "Keep him safe. I will find you in the next life."

They kissed and clasped each other as the temperature around them dropped. Finally, Conor tore himself away and ran for the cabin door.

Saoirse turned to face Eric, the two of them the only ones not lashed down.

"Will you trust me, Saoirse?" he asked.

"Do I have a choice?"

He transformed into an ebony stallion to the shrieks of the crew. When he lay down, she mounted his back.

"Your mother loves you; always remember, my son," Saoirse called on the wind. The gale whipped water into her hair. Cailleach Bhéara had been waiting patiently. The immortal representation of winter, the sea hag knew to wait as only a season of the year could.

The tempest was upon them.

"Ride!" she shouted. In their unspoken exchange, she knew he would take her away from Conor and Nolan, and the ship would survive if she were not on it. Tears streamed from her cheeks, and she choked back heavy sobs as he ran across the waters. Great waves rose up. She fought for air.

He leaped higher. The action knocked the remaining air from her lungs. She wrapped his ebony hair around her wrists and clung to his back. When there was air, she breathed deeply before another huge wave broke over them. The higher he ran, the colder she became. Her fingers were numb and slipping. Her breathing was shallow, and her breaths were few. She was falling into the mouths of the hungry black waves.

Eric did not give up on her. She felt his warm arms, in human form, embrace her and protect her head from the rocks. In the darkness and water, without air, she was drowning.

She rode her mare by moonlight. She was dancing in the rain. Nolan's first steps. Her son dancing. The warmth in Conor's smile. His embrace.

"Saoirse, breathe!" Eric screamed as they broke through the stormy waters. She could not. Her spirit was drifting away on the sea foam. "Saoirse, please come back!"

"*Saoirse!*" he cried as he held her head above the waves.

The waters began to recede, and the clouds cleared. She was free.

Conor and Nolan's journey continues in . . .

A MONKEY'S MASK

SEVEN YEARS LATER, ON THE COAST OF LANKADIPA LOCATED IN THE SOUTH TROPICAL SEAS

Palm trees. Sandy beach. Bonfires. Laughter and song. Conor sat drinking with the chief and his men. He found it strange that the atmosphere reminded him so much of an Eirann gathering. Someone struck the bohdran and drums while a set of flutes joined, followed by a setar. Sweet music played into the star-filled night. Always, the sound of waves hitting the shore. The tide would be coming in soon. A woman began to sing. The instruments slowed to match her lament.

Conor drank the fermented coconut water the locals called 'toddy'. It was light, refreshing even. He didn't realize he was drunk until he stood and stumbled to find a lonely tree that he could water. Out of politeness to his company, he headed up and away along the path to the village, looking for a secluded spot.

Conor suspected not all was as it was made out to be. The women of the village had a good say in the local matters, for one. He had seen them arguing with the chief about how it was. Was the chief even a chief? He could not tell. Mostly, the villagers were too adept. Always there to refill his cup. Always watching. No wastrels or layabouts amongst this group. The ones who wore masks, what were they hiding? It had not been like this the last time he visited. For one, the guards hadn't worn masks. He had seen that they were human, not the famed yaksha or raksha that gave him nightmares. A man was not meant to be so long in the tooth without a good reason. Conor would pay good coin to find out.

He found the right tree before his bladder burst. Standing on a floor of coconut husks, he wondered if taking a wet dump would be a challenge. Better on solid ground, he concluded. Catching his balance on the shells, he had just lowered his sarong when a dart whipped past his left ear, sticking itself to the tree.

"Hey!" He turned around, hands up to show he would not make trouble. "I'm unarmed. You have me. Who is there and what do you want?" He may have slurred some of the words.

Silence. Waves crashing on the shore.

"I'm right here. Do your worst!" He could hear whispering from the bushes. Voices in a tongue that were beyond his understanding. "Now, you're making me angry," Conor growled. "Come on, do your worst!" That seemed to decide them. He looked down to find a dart sticking into his chest. "Well, thank you." He collapsed.

Conor woke up in a field of green. His ears worked first. Neighing, grunts, out breaths, horses. He slowly opened a crusty eye. Hooves. His shoulders ached. His legs ached worse. Worse yet was his head. This, he knew, was from the drink. His arms were bound hand to foot. He was not a flexible man. He was not meant to stretch so. He let out a groan.

He couldn't hear the sea. Sudden panic. In this land, if you couldn't hear the sea, you were inland. One law of Lankadipa drummed into everyone was that *foreigners outside the boundaries of the harbour are forbidden to leave except by death.* He rolled, feeling his hands land in something warm and squishy. *Horse turds. What is going on?*

"You should know your limits, asura." The voice was male and a high tenor. Conor did not recognize it. "You're kind are not welcome on our shores."

"I'm no asura," Conor said. He wasn't sure if the voice was listening.

"You are fair of skin and sport the red hair. We

were warned that you would come and that you would come to destabilize us."

"Wait, what?! I think you have me confused with someone else, and he is not that sort." Conor's heart sank. They thought he was Sinha. *Ignorant bastards couldn't tell an asura from a man if their life depended on it.* Would they kill him knowing that he wasn't their intended target? He heard again the voices arguing in a tongue he could not understand. The men finally seemed to make up their minds. He felt himself lifted as a cloth was dropped over his head from behind. The air was knocked out of him as he was hauled like a bag onto a horse's back. *Please put me back*, he prayed. A moment later, he was senseless.

For news on upcoming book releases and a sneak peek at what happens behind the scenes, sign up for D.M De Alwis' newsletter at dmdealwis.com.

A Word from D.M. De Alwis:

Thank you for reading A WATER HORSE. I hope you enjoyed it.

While writing A MONKEY'S MASK, I was inspired by Englishman Robert Knox's account of two decades of captivity in Sri Lanka in the 1600s. A WATER HORSE is the backstory for how Conor and Nolan end up in the South Tropical Seas to be kidnapped by a King of Lanka. Their story continues in A MONKEY'S MASK.

Also from the same universe is the Pawn of Samsara Duology, available from major booksellers.

In A LION'S HEAD, the gods have migrated humans to the immortal realm of the asura. Wishing to return his people home, the water buffalo deity Isha binds himself to the tyrant. Meanwhile, the man-lion Sinha—aided by three human companions—accepts a quest to kill the king.

In A LION'S PRIDE, the asura shape-shifter Sinha travels to the mortal realm in search of reincarnates of his past companions. When hungry ghosts and demons begin to roam the mortal realm unchecked, he is drawn into a feud between two religious factions, while his ancient enemy plots revenge.

About the Author

D. M. De Alwis is a Canadian Indie author with a passion for researching and writing prehistoric South Asian fantasy. D.M.'s novels are bursting with insight leading to the answer to the ultimate question of life, the universe, and Everything. Her novels are edited by Elise Abram and published by Ahasae Tharu Publishing. To find out more, check out her musings at dmdealwis.com or follow her on Threads, BlueSky or Instagram (@dmdealwis).

Enjoy this book?

Help others find A WATER HORSE by leaving a review on
StoryGraph, Goodreads,
Amazon, or wherever you buy books.

Better yet . . . request these books from
your local library!